THE BIRTHDAY KITTEN

"We've waited so long," said Terry mournfully. "We're almost nine – and except for a hedgehog I kept out in the garden shed one winter, and a robin with a broken leg we kept till it mended, we've never had a proper pet."

"I suppose, then, Mummy, it *isn't* any good putting down a puppy or kitten on our list?" said Tessie.

"Not while Baby is small," said her mother. "I don't want to trip over animals when I'm carrying Baby about."

Other Enid Blyton titles
available in Beaver

The Birthday Kitten

Enid Blyton

*Illustrated by Joyce Smith
and David Dowland*

Beaver Books

A Beaver Book
Published by Arrow Books Limited
62-65 Chandos Place, London WC2N 4NW

An imprint of Century Hutchinson Limited

London Melbourne Sydney Auckland
Johannesburg and agencies throughout
the world

First published by Lutterworth Press 1958
Sparrow edition 1980
Reprinted 1983
Beaver edition 1984
Reprinted 1987 and 1988

Printed and bound in Great Britain by
Anchor Brendon Limited, Tiptree, Essex

ISBN 0 09 924100 5

CONTENTS

1. "WHAT DO YOU WANT FOR YOUR BIRTHDAY?"

"TWINS! You'd better begin to think what you want for your birthday!" said Mummy. "Granny was asking me what you'd like yesterday—and Auntie Sue asked me today."

"Oh! Yes, we'll think of our list straight away!" said Terry. "Come on, Tessie. I've got my pencil. Now—we want some new snap-cards, don't we? Ours are so dirty!"

"Yes. And I'd love a new pencil-box," said Tessie. "Someone dropped mine at school the other day, and the lid broke."

Terry wrote "Tessie" at the top of one side of his piece of paper, and "Terry" on the other. "Now," he said, "that's PENCIL-BOX for you, Tessie—and I'll put SNAP-CARDS down for me. And I want a book too—about animals." He wrote that down under his own name.

"I'd like a book about birds," said Tessie. "And I know the one I want. I saw it in a book-shop the other day. I'll write down the title for you."

"It would be a good idea to put BOOK-

TOKENS too," said Terry, nibbling the end of his pencil. "Mummy, can we put BOOK-TOKENS? Sometimes Granpa gives us such a dull book, and it's a waste of reading then. But if he gave us a book-token it means we can go round the book-shop by ourselves and choose what we really like."

"Of course put that down," said Mummy. "You always choose sensible books. But put a few other things besides those you've already written, Terry. You won't get everything you want, but at least there will be plenty for people to choose from."

"Well, let's put down a new doll for you, Tessie, and a new clockwork car for me," said Terry. "And what about a jigsaw or some other game? And I'd love some paints."

The lists grew quite long. Terry whispered to Tessie and she nodded.

"What are you whispering about?" asked Mummy, smiling. "Something special?"

"Yes," said Terry. "I was wondering if it's any use putting down what we *always* put down and never get, Mummy."

"What's that?" asked his mother.

"Well—we *always* put down a puppy or a

kitten," said Terry. "Always. But we've never had one yet."

"Last Christmas I put down PUPPY three times on my list," said Tessie, "and I got one— but it was a *toy* one! Just a nightdress case that

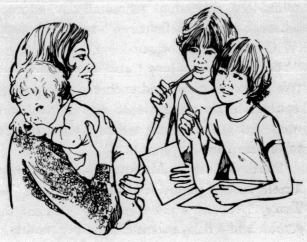

"I don't really want any animals"

holds my nightie beautifully—but I want a *live* one. Or a kitten—I don't mind which!"

"*Is* it any good putting down puppy or kitten again, Mummy?" said Terry.

"Well—I don't really want any animals till Baby is bigger," said Mummy. "And then, you know, they cost money to feed if you are going to keep them properly—and a dog needs a kennel, because I couldn't have him in the house while Baby is so small."

"I don't see *why*," began Tessie. "*We* could look after him. I'd love to."

"Darling, you are at school all day, except in the week-ends and holidays," said her mother. "Wait till Baby is bigger."

"We've waited so long," said Terry mournfully. "We're almost nine—and except for a hedgehog I kept out in the garden shed one winter, and a robin with a broken leg we kept till it mended, we've never had a proper pet."

"I suppose, then, Mummy, it *isn't* any good putting down a puppy or kitten on our list?" said Tessie.

"Not while Baby is small," said her mother. "I don't want to trip over animals when I'm carrying Baby about. What about putting down a canary? You could have that, if you like to look after it properly each day."

"Yes. That's a good idea. We'll put down canary," said Terry, and wrote it down under both their names in big letters "CANARY". "It doesn't matter which of us has it, we can share it. I only hope we get a cage with it!"

It seemed a long time before their birthday came. They always shared one between them because they were twins. Their mother made them a marvellous cake. She was icing it in the kitchen when they came running in from school one afternoon.

"Oh, go out of the kitchen, quickly!" said Mummy. "You mustn't see your cake yet! Terry, look in the dining-room cupboard for me, please, and see if you can find a packet of tiny birthday-cake candles. Count out eighteen—nine for each of you—and bring them to me."

"Birthdays *are* exciting!" said Tessie as she went with Terry to the dining-room. "Terry—do you think we're going to have a puppy or kitten—or perhaps a canary?"

"I don't know," said Terry, hunting in the cupboard. "I haven't heard a whine or a bark or a mew or a trill at all, not *anywhere* in the house. Have you?"

"No. I haven't," said Tessie. "Isn't it a pity we're so very fond of animals and haven't any—and Bill over the road has a dog and rabbits and mice—and really doesn't like them much. He's always forgetting to feed them. It doesn't seem fair."

"Lots of things aren't fair," said Terry. "But you just can't do anything about it! Here are the candles at last—in this corner. I'll count out eighteen into your hand, Tessie. Fancy—eighteen —isn't it a lot! I'm glad we're twins and have a double birthday."

They took the candles back to Mother—and just as they were going out of the kitchen, they heard a funny squeak! They stopped at once and looked at one another.

"A puppy!" whispered Terry. "I'm sure it was! Listen!"

They stood in the hall and listened again. Squeak! Squeeeak! Squeeeeak!

"Well—it may not be a puppy—but it's something alive!" said Terry. "It doesn't really *sound* like a puppy—or a kitten either, really."

Tessie went to look out of the hall window. "The noise seems to come from outside somewhere," she said. "There—I heard it again!"

They listened eagerly. And then Tessie gave a heavy sigh and said "Oh!" in such a miserable voice that Terry was astonished. "What's the matter?" he said.

"Can't you see what's making the squeak?" said Tessie, disappointed. "Look—it's our back-gate! It's swinging to and fro in the wind, and squeaking each time."

"Horrible old gate!" said Terry, very disappointed too. "I'll go out and oil you this minute—pretending to be a puppy, and squeaking just like one!"

"Cheer up!" said Tessie. "It's our birthday tomorrow, and even if we *don't* get a kitten or a puppy, we'll have lots of other things. I vote we go to bed early tonight to make the birthday come quicker!"

"Well, if we don't get *some* pet between us tomorrow, I'll—I'll—well, I don't know *what* I'll do!" said Terry. "Something FIERCE!"

2

"AREN'T THERE
ANY MORE PRESENTS?"

THE twins' mother came into their bedroom the next morning, and drew the curtains. "Happy birthday, twins!" she said. "Even the sun has decided to make it a nice day for you!"

She gave them each a birthday hug and a kiss. "All your presents are waiting for you downstairs," she said. "So I know you'll dress at top speed this morning! WHAT a good thing it's Saturday, and there's no school today! Well, well —to think you're nine years old—and in your tenth year already! You *are* growing up!"

The twins washed and dressed at top speed. As they dressed they heard the postman come. What a loud ratta-tat-TAT he gave! "He must have a lot of cards for us, and perhaps some parcels!" said Terry. "Oh, *where's* my other sock! I'm longing to go downstairs."

The postman had certainly brought them a lot of cards! Eight for each of them, and four between them as well. And there were four parcels besides, all looking very exciting in their brown paper.

On the breakfast table were other parcels, this
time wrapped up in pretty birthday paper, not
brown paper. "Hello, twins!" said Daddy, and
gave them a birthday hug each. "Many happy returns of the day! How does it feel to be nine?"

"Well—no different from yesterday, really,"
said Terry. "I always *think* there'll be a difference,
but there isn't. Mummy, may we open our
parcels?"

"Two each before breakfast—and the rest afterwards," said his mother. The twins looked at the
parcels. It was quite clear that none of them held a
puppy or a kitten! But perhaps one was waiting
outside! Once when they had had a tricycle given
to them, it had been out in the yard. A puppy
might quite well be out there too—in a box, or
even a kennel!

They chose two big parcels and opened them in
excitement.

"I *say*! Look at this ship!" said Terry, his eyes
shining. "And I didn't even put it down on my
list. Who gave it to me? OH! Isn't it a beauty.
Daddy, may I sail it on the pond this afternoon?"

"I should think so," said Daddy. "Look, there's
the card to say who gave it to you."

Terry looked at it. It said "Lots of love from

Daddy." He ran at his father and gave him a real bear-hug. "Daddy—*you* gave it to me. Oh, it's a beauty. Tom's got one too, but his is only half the size of this one. Oh, what shall I call it?"

"LOOK what I've got," said Tessie, suddenly. She had been undoing one of her biggest parcels too. "A doll's cot! Mummy, I know it's from you, I know it is! You said the other day that my baby doll ought to sleep in a cot! Oh, Mummy, it's lovely! I can buy some blankets and sheets and a pillow for it if I get any birthday money."

"Look and see what *Granny's* given you before you do that," said Mummy, and Tessie hurriedly undid the other big parcel.

"Oh, Granny's given me everything for the cot!" she said in delight. "Look Mummy—there's even a little eiderdown! Oh won't my baby doll be pleased?"

Terry had undone his second parcel now—and he couldn't for the life of him think what it was. It was a long curved piece of wood, smooth to the touch, and sharp at the edges.

"Oh—*I* know what it is!" he said. "It's that funny thing they throw in Australia—that comes back to your hand—what's it called now?"

"A boomerang," said Daddy. "Yes, Uncle

Roddy has sent it from Australia—he bought it specially for you. You'll be able to practise with it in the garden—throw it at one of the apple trees and knock off the ripest apple at the top!"

"You really must have your breakfast now," said Mummy. "Then you can open your other parcels. Sit down, twins."

The twins sat down to their boiled eggs, gazing at the ship, the boomerang, the doll's cot and the cot-clothes. What fun they were going to have with them—and there were still plenty of parcels to undo. Really, a birthday was very exciting!

But still at the back of their minds was a little worrying thought—*was* there going to be a puppy or kitten—or not? That would be much the nicest present of all—something alive, that they could love and that would love them. They listened for any bark or mew from outside—but they couldn't hear anything.

They opened the rest of their presents after breakfast. A magnificent new pencil-box for Tessie, filled with pencils, pens, crayons and two rubbers—an enormous jigsaw between them both —snap-cards for Terry—a book for each of them from Granpa—and hurrah, they were the books they wanted.

They opened the rest of their presents

"Mine's all about birds—the very one I was looking at in the book-shop the other day!" said Tessie. "Good old Granpa! It's a beauty! And oh —you've got the animal book *you* wanted, Terry. Bags I read it after you! What super pictures!"

There was a tin of toffees for each of them, a clockwork car for Terry, and a lovely little Spanish doll for Tessie.

"I know who she's from!" said Tessie, in delight. "Auntie Kate—because she went to Spain for her holiday and *told* me she'd brought back my birthday present from there! Mummy, I shall call this doll Juanita, and stand her on the mantelpiece, because she's good enough for an ornament! She's too smart to cuddle!"

The twins were really delighted with all their presents. They set them out on the floor and gloated over them.

"Clear up the paper and string, dears," said Mummy. "And I'll clear away the breakfast."

"Mummy—there aren't any *more* presents, are there?" asked Terry, still hopeful that there might be something alive, even if it was only a canary.

"Good gracious, dear—how many more do you want!" said Mummy, stacking the plates together. "You've been very, very lucky."

"There aren't any out in the yard this time, are there?" said Tessie. "You know—like our tricycle was once."

"*No*, darling," said Mummy. "You sound quite greedy! Now go and kiss Baby—she's not old enough to know it's your birthday, but you must kiss her all the same!"

The twins went off to the little room where Baby slept by herself. She was awake and kicking all the clothes off.

"We didn't have a puppy or a kitten after all," said Terry, mournfully, as they looked down at the smiling baby.

"I know—and I'm awfully disappointed that we haven't even got a canary," said Tessie. "I'd much rather have had that than that lovely doll's cot. Still—we've got Baby Anne—she's really *quite* a pet, isn't she?"

"Yes. She's a darling," said Terry. "And *she'd* love a puppy too, I know she would. Oh well— let's go and put our cards up round our bedrooms. We really have been very lucky, you know!"

3.
"OH QUICK—
DO SOMETHING!"

THE twins enjoyed their birthday morning very much. After they had done their usual little jobs—making their beds, sweeping and dusting their rooms, and running Saturday errands for their mother, they were free to play with their new toys.

"I'd really like to sail my ship," said Terry, looking at it longingly. "I was going to sail it this afternoon, but our party begins at half-past three, doesn't it, Mummy?"

"Yes, dear—and you'll have to blow up the balloons for me," said Mummy, "and bring some bedroom chairs down for the dining-room because we shan't have enough. And I want Tessie to pick some flowers out of the garden and arrange them in the vases for me, to make the rooms look nice."

"Mummy, we'll do all that, of course," said Terry. "But it really won't take us long. Couldn't we take my boat to sail on the pond this morning?"

"I want to make up my new doll's cot," said Tessie. "It will be such fun to make the bed for the first time and put that little pink eiderdown on top. My baby doll is very, very pleased with it, Mummy!"

Mummy laughed. "I'm sure she is. Well, look now, why don't you do all my little jobs, and make your doll's cot up quickly—and then go to the pond with Terry? He really is longing to sail his ship. You'll want some string, Terry, because the pond is big, and if the wind blows hard, it might take your ship right out into the middle of the water."

"I've got some string," said Terry, patting his pocket. "Plenty. All right—we'll buck up and do everything, Mummy, and then go to the pond. Can we take Baby with us in her pram?"

"No. Not by the pond," said Mummy. "I do trust you, you know that—but it would be dreadful if the pram ran down into the pond. I'll keep Baby here."

It wasn't long before the twins had done everything, and Tessie had made up her new cot beautifully, and put the baby doll into it. She looked very peaceful, lying there with her eyes shut.

Baby Anne was in her pram, lying peacefully with *her* eyes shut too. Tessie wished they could take her to the pond—she did so like being with them. She picked up Baby's soft yellow duck, and put it near her hand.

"She loves it, but she's always throwing it away!" said Tessie. "I've picked it up about a hundred times, I should think! Are you ready, Terry? Is your new ship heavy to carry? It's so big!"

"I don't care how heavy it is," said Terry, proudly. "I *like* carrying it! Won't all the children stare when we meet them. Come on, Tessie."

The other children certainly did stare when they saw the big ship Terry was carrying. Harry came up and wanted to carry it for him. But Terry wouldn't let him. Nobody else was going to carry his birthday ship that day!

It was quite a long way to the pond. They had to go up the hill and down again, round a corner, and then, lying at the edge of the field, there was the pond.

It was a nice big one, and it usually had ducks on it, but this morning there were none. It was fairly deep in the middle, and would have been nicer if only people hadn't thrown rubbish into it. There was a tin kettle, two old cans and a wooden box that bobbed up and down. They spoilt the pretty little pond.

"Well, now we'll see how my new ship sails!" said Terry, in delight. "I've decided to call her *Flying Swan*, Tessie. Do you think that's a good name?"

"Oh *yes*," said Tessie. "Ships do look rather like swans when they're sailing. It's a nice name."

Soon the ship was on the pond. It floated beautifully, and didn't flop on its side at all, as some ships do.

"Look at her!" said Terry, in delight. "See how she bobs over the little ripples! Look how the wind is filling her sails just like a real ship! She's speeding over the water exactly like those ships we saw down at the seaside."

The ship really was a fine sight to watch. She sailed over the pond right to the very end of her string, and then, when Terry pulled at her gently, she turned and came back again, as steady as could be!

"Let me hold her now," said Tessie, and Terry gave her the string. Tessie liked to feel the ship pulling at her hand as she sailed here and there. "She feels alive when the string pulls on my finger," she said. "Oh look, Terry—is one of her sails coming loose? Yes, look—it's gone all crooked."

"Let me have the string," said Terry at once. "I expect a knot has come loose." He took the string from Tessie, and pulled the boat in carefully.

"Yes—it's just a knot that wants tying up," he said. "Let's go and sit down by that bush and I can do it properly."

So they took the ship to the big bush and sat down. The knot was very awkward to tie, and the two children bent their heads over the ship, lost in what they were doing.

They didn't see a big boy come up and look all round. He didn't see them either, for the bush hid them, and they were not making a sound. He carried a small parcel, something tied up in an old flour bag. He had it hidden under his jacket.

He didn't come right down to the pond, but stood a little way away, still looking cautiously all round. Then he raised his arm and threw the flour bag straight over the water of the pond.

"SPLASH!"

The noise made the twins lift their heads at once and stare at the pond. "What was that?" asked Terry. "What fell into the water just then?"

"I don't know," said Tessie, puzzled. "I didn't see anything. And there's nobody about. Perhaps it was a fish or a frog jumping."

"Look—what's that over there—in the middle of the pond?" said Terry. "It's something moving. Whatever can it be?"

Then a noise came to their ears—a high-pitched squeak, and the thing in the pond began to roll over and over.

"Look—see that bag, or whatever it is?" said Terry, leaping up. "That's what fell—or was thrown in—and there's something in it, Tessie! Something alive!"

"Oh quick, then do something!" cried Tessie. "It will drown! See how it's struggling—but it can't get out of the bag!"

Terry tore off his shoes and socks and waded into the water. The bottom of the pond was muddy and his feet sank into it as he waded. The water soon came over his

What could it be?

knees—but at last he managed to reach out to the struggling thing near him, and picked it up. At once he felt a wriggling, frantic little body inside. What could it be? What *could* it be?

4

"WE REALLY
MUST *GET HELP*"

"TESSIE! There's something inside this bag!" cried Terry. "It feels like some tiny animal. Oh, how *could* anyone do such a cruel thing! Fancy tying it up and then throwing it away to drown!"

He waded to shore, holding the wriggling little thing in the bag as gently as he could. It struggled and squeaked in terror.

"What is it? Oh, Terry, poor little thing! Undo the knots tying up the bag!" cried Tessie. "Who threw it into the pond? I never saw anyone come— I only heard the splash."

"I can't undo these knots," said Terry, sitting down to try again. "The string is so wet. Put your hand into my left-hand pocket. Tessie, and get out my knife for me."

Tessie did as she was told, and handed him his knife, opening the blade for him first. He took it and cut the string. The mouth of the old flour bag fell open—and a tiny white tail appeared.

"Look—there's its tail!" said Tessie. "What a tiny creature—no bigger than a rat. It isn't a white rat, is it, Terry? Be careful the poor thing doesn't bite you."

"I'll take it out very carefully," said Terry. "It's so terrified—and so weak too, now. I expect it's half-drowned!"

Very gently indeed he pulled the tiny creature out of the dripping wet bag. At first the children couldn't make out what it was, it was so wet and draggled and small. Then a tiny mew came from the little thing, and they both knew at once what it was.

"A *kitten!* A tiny, tiny kitten," said Tessie. "A white one. Oh, poor little thing, it's so frightened. It can't be more than two or three weeks old. Has it got its eyes open? It's so wet and miserable, I can't see."

"We'd better take it home and dry it at once," said Terry. "It ought to be put somewhere warm, it's shivering. What a pity the sun's just gone in! Oh, poor little frightened thing, we'll do what we can for you!"

"Give it to me," said Tessie. "I'll dry it gently with my hanky—and then I'll put it inside my jersey and hold it there. It will be warm then. What a tiny, tiny mew it has!"

Terry gave the kitten to her, and watched his

sister dry the little thing with her handkerchief. It didn't seem to like it much, and mewed again. But it liked it when Tessie put it carefully under her soft woollen jersey and held it there safely. It stopped mewing at once.

"You get your ship," said Tessie. "We left it there, by the bush. You don't want to sail it any more, do you?"

"No," said Terry. "I want to get this kitten home and safe. What do you think Mummy will say, Tessie?"

Tessie was silent. What *would* Mummy say? She didn't want pets in the house while she

had Baby to carry about, up and down stairs; and certainly it would be dreadful if she fell over a kitten on the stairs, with Baby in her arms. But how could they do anything but take it home?

"We can't tell

"What a tiny mew!"   Mummy *today*,"

said Terry. "She has a lot to do, because it's our birthday, and there's our party this afternoon."

"Well—where can we put the kitten then?" said Tessie. "Not in the house, because Mummy would hear it squeaking. It would have to be somewhere outside."

"Let's put it in the old shed," said Terry. "Nobody ever goes there except us, now Daddy has built a new shed. There's only just our tricycles there, and our old spades and things. We could make a bed for the kitten there."

"What about feeding it?" said Tessie. "How do we feed it? How old is it, I wonder? Its mother still ought to be feeding it, oughtn't she? Oh dear—what a lot of difficulties there are!"

"Isn't there anyone we can ask?" wondered Terry. "Someone who knows about animals? We've never had any, so we really don't know. What about Harry? His father is an animal doctor, isn't he? What's he called now—a vet?"

"Yes," said Tessie. "A vet. He went to Farmer Hill when his horses were ill—and he mended the leg of Mrs. Brown's dog, when he got run over—and he took a thorn out of Hilary's cat's front paw. I was there when he did that. He's nice. Yes, let's ask Harry if he knows anything about tiny kittens."

"Well—if *my* father was an animal doctor, I'd know a lot about animals!" said Terry. "I'd love to learn. Let's go to Harry's house and see if he's in."

So they went to Harry Williams' house and walked round the back to find him. Terry was still carrying his big ship, of course, and Tessie had the kitten cuddled under her jersey. It had stopped squeaking now, because it was beginning to feel warm.

Harry was playing in his garden. "Hallo!" he said, in surprise. "What have you come for—to show me that ship? My word, isn't it a real beauty?"

"No. We came to ask if you knew anything about tiny kittens," said Terry. "Someone threw one into the pond when we were there with my ship—and I waded in and got it. It's so wet and cold and miserable. We thought perhaps you'd know how we could feed it."

"No, *I* don't," said Harry. "But the kennel-maid who helps my father with the dogs here would tell you."

"Will you ask her?" said Tessie.

A sly look came into Harry's eyes. "Yes—if you lend me your ship to sail," he said.

"I can't do that!" said Terry. "I only had it to-day, for my birthday!"

"Well, I shan't ask the kennel-maid for you, then," said Harry. "Why don't you ask your mother? She'd know."

"She doesn't want us to have animals yet, till our baby is bigger," explained Tessie. "Harry, don't be mean—the tiny thing is so frightened and miserable. We simply *must* get advice."

"Well, tell Terry to lend me his ship and I'll go straight and ask the kennel-maid," said Harry.

Terry gave Harry the ship when he saw Tessie's

"Lend me your ship to sail"

eyes filling with tears. He never could bear to see his twin sister upset. "All right. Here you are," he said. "But you're *mean*. I shall get into a row with my father if he finds I've lent my ship to someone. Now go and ask the kennel-maid."

"You come with me," said Harry, taking the big ship in delight. "My word—isn't she a beauty? Has she a name?"

"The *Flying Swan*," said Terry, in an angry voice. He thought Harry was really horrid.

"Pooh—what a silly name! I shall call her *Snow-Maiden*," said Harry.

"You won't! She's *my* ship," said Terry, but Harry only laughed. "Come on—bring the kitten," he said. "What a lot of fuss you make about a silly half-drowned creature! Look — there's Miss Morgan, the kennel-maid. Go and ask her what you want to!" And off he ran—carrying Terry's lovely ship with him!

MISS Morgan, the kennel-maid, was very
busy. She had four dogs on leads, and
was putting them into their kennels. She
talked to them as she shut them in.

"Now you be good, all of you—and Tinker, it's
no use your barking the place down, you'll only
upset the others. I'll take you all for another run
this afternoon if you're quiet. And don't you try
and bite that bandage off your leg, Lassie—be a
good dog now!"

The twins waited until she had shut up all the
dogs safely. They thought she sounded sensible
and kind, and when she turned round they saw
that she had a merry, smiling face.

"Hallo!" she said. "What do *you* want? Have
you come to see the vet? He's out."

"No. We came to see Harry really," said Terry,
"to ask him if he knew what we could do to help
a half-drowned kitten—and he said we could ask
you for advice."

"A half-drowned kitten—whatever have you
been doing to the poor thing?" said Miss Morgan,

as Tessie drew it gently out from the warmth of
her jersey.

"Nothing!" said Terry. "*We* didn't try to
drown it! Someone came to the pond when we
were sailing our ship and threw a bag into the
water—and we saw the bag wriggling—and I
waded out to it . . ."

She shut up all the dogs safely

"And when we undid the bag, there was this
tiny wet kitten inside, choking and spluttering,"
said Tessie. "It was so frightened and cold."

"Poor wee thing," said Miss Morgan, and took
it gently from Tessie's hands. "It's in a bad way.
It's been half-starved by the look of it—and see,

there's something wrong with one of its back legs."

"PLEASE tell us what to do with it," said Tessie, in tears. "Will it live?"

"Oh yes, I think so," said Miss Morgan. "It's not shivering now—and by the sound of its little mew, it's very hungry. I'll show you how to feed it."

She took them into the little bare surgery, where the vet saw all his animal patients, and went to a cupboard. She handed Terry a small fountain-pen filler. "There's some warm milk in that saucepan over there," she said. "I've been feeding a puppy with it, but there's enough left for this tiny mite. Put some in the glass filler, will you?"

Terry put the glass end of the filler into the saucepan of milk, squeezed the rubber end, and drew milk into the filler. Miss Morgan took it from him.

"Open your mouth, kitty," she said, and put the filler gently against the kitten's mouth. A drop of milk ran in, and the kitten swallowed it. It mewed.

"Yes—it liked that," said Miss Morgan. "Well, take a few more drops, kitty—you'll soon feel better!"

The twins watched Miss Morgan feeding the tiny creature, and were delighted to see how eagerly it swallowed the milk. Terry filled the little pen-filler twice more, and was allowed to feed the kitten himself. Then Tessie had a turn.

"Well, that's how you must feed it, until it can lap," said Miss Morgan. "Have you a filler at home? I can give you one if you haven't."

"Yes, Tessie's got one," said Terry. "How shall we know when the kitten is ready to lap, Miss Morgan?"

"It will lick a drop of milk off your finger then," said Miss Morgan. "As soon as it does that, you can teach it to lap from a saucer. It will soon learn!"

"Its eyes aren't open," said Tessie. "Is it very, very young?"

"It's very, very *small*," said Miss Morgan, "small enough for its eyes still not to be open— but I think it's older than it looks. I expect it hasn't opened its eyes because it's weak and neglected. Are you sure you can look after it?"

The twins nodded. "Yes!" said Terry. "We can —we mean to, anyway. Who else would, if we didn't?"

"What about its leg?" asked Tessie, anxiously.

"The leg that hangs limp and doesn't move."

"I think that will get all right," said Miss Morgan. "But if not, you can bring it back to me again. Now—keep the kitten somewhere warm—it will probably have felt shocked and chilled, when it struggled in the cold pond water! I'm glad you were there to save it."

She gave the tiny thing to Tessie, who put it back under her warm jersey again. "It's more like a white rat than a kitten!" said Miss Morgan. "But it should grow up into a pretty little thing. Take it home now."

"Do we—do we have to pay you anything for helping us?" asked Terry. "I did lend Harry my birthday ship, but you've done such a lot. We've got some birthday money you could have."

"Bless you!" said Miss Morgan, smiling her nice smile. "I'm glad to help, and there isn't even a penny to pay. It's your birthday, is it? Many happy returns of the day! You've had a very unexpected birthday present, haven't you—a half-drowned kitten!"

The twins set off down the path. "She's nice, isn't she?" said Tessie. "Let's buy her some sweets sometime. I feel better about the kitten now, don't you? If it can take milk so easily it will soon be all right. It feels so nice against me, under my jersey."

"Tessie—do you think we'd *better* put it into the shed while it's so tiny?" asked Terry, as they walked off down the road. "And don't you think we ought to give it milk in the middle of the night? You know, Mother gives Baby her bottle quite a lot of times, doesn't she, morning, afternoon and night—and *early* in the morning too!"

"Well—we can't possibly creep out of the house in the middle of the night to feed the kitten," said Tessie.

"No, we can't," said Terry. "Perhaps we'd better find somewhere near our bedrooms. What about the little boxroom? If the kitten made a noise no one would hear it there—and it's next to our bedrooms."

"Yes. We could keep it there till it doesn't need feeding at night," said Tessie, cheering up. "Oh dear—I DO wish we could tell Mummy about it. Can't we possibly?"

"No. It would be mean of us to ask her to do something on our birthday that she's already refused to do," said Terry. "She might think she'd *got* to have the kitten, and then it would be a nuisance instead of something lovely. I think we can manage all right, Tessie."

"But what about when it grows big?" said Tessie.

"Don't let's bother about that yet," said Terry. "We could give it away, I expect. The thing is we've got to be kind to it *now*, and get it well and happy. Here we are—now be careful nobody sees us, and asks you what that bump is under your jumper!"

They went quietly to the back door and peeped in. Nobody was there. They tiptoed in, and went quietly up the stairs. "We'll go straight to the box-room," whispered Terry.

And then they heard Mummy's voice! "Is that you, twins? I wondered whatever had happened to you! Come and tell me what you've been doing this birthday morning!"

"WHAT A GOOD IDEA!"

THE twins looked at one another in dismay, and Tessie clutched the kitten more closely to her, hoping it would not make the tiniest sound.

"You pop upstairs quickly," said Terry, "and find a place to put the kitten. I'll go in and talk to Mummy."

Tessie raced upstairs. She went into the tiny boxroom. The hot-water pipes ran through it, so it was nice and warm. "Just the place for a cold little kitten!" thought Tessie. "Now—what shall I give it for a bed?"

There was nowhere in the boxroom that would be soft and comfortable. Tessie wondered what to use for a cosy little bed—and then she suddenly thought of something. Yes! Her new doll's cot! It would be just the right size for the kitten.

She ran into the playroom. The cot stood beside the toy cupboard, and the little baby doll was lying in it, with her eyes closed. Tessie lifted her out and put her on a chair.

"This will be just right for you, kitten!" she said, and went back into the little boxroom with the cot. She set it down in a corner and turned back the cot-clothes. She took out the sheets and left the little blanket, the pillow and the pink eiderdown. She put the tiny kitten on to the blanket and covered it up with the eiderdown.

"There!" she said. "Now you lie there and sleep, kitten—and don't make any noise! You'll be quite safe here, because nobody ever comes into this room."

She heard footsteps running up the stairs. It was Terry. "Tessie —where are you? Is everything all right?"

"Yes—come and look!" said Tessie, and took Terry into the boxroom. He laughed when he saw the tiny kitten in the cot.

"What a good idea! But that won't be big enough for it when it gets older. It could have my

"It's fast asleep"

toy garage then, with a blanket inside—or the brick-box!"

"It's fast asleep," said Tessie. "It's quite dry now—look, its fur is beginning to look nice and soft. How *could* anyone throw such a dear little thing away?"

"When do you think we ought to feed it again?" asked Terry. "It's almost dinner-time now for us. Shall we feed it afterwards?"

"Yes. Baby always leaves a little warm milk in her bottle," said Tessie. "We can use that. Where's that little glass filler of mine?"

"I saw it in your old pencil-box," said Terry. "I'll go and look. We'd better keep the boxroom door shut, Tessie, in case anyone hears the little thing mewing."

They went down to their dinner. It was nice to have a secret, but it would have been nicer still to share it with Mummy and Daddy!

"Well, birthday children!" said Daddy. "Are you looking forward to your party? I see there is a magnificent cake out in the kitchen!"

"Yes—with eighteen candles on it!" said Tessie. "Goodness—when we're eighteen, there'll have to be thirty-six, won't there, Mummy?"

After dinner Mummy had to give Baby her

bottle. "Shall I give it to her for you, Mummy?" asked Tessie. "I know you're busy. I've fed her before, so you know you can trust me."

"All right—you may if you're very careful," said Mummy: "I'll get Baby for you, and settle her on your knee, and then prepare her bottle."

So, very soon, there was Tessie sitting in Mummy's low nursing-chair, proudly giving Baby Anne her bottle! Terry came to see. "If she leaves any milk, let me have it for the kitten," he said. "It will be nice and warm."

"Well, get the milk jug from my dolls' tea-set," said Tessie. "I can pour it quickly in there, when Baby has finished."

Terry fetched the little jug. Baby seemed very hungry and was sucking at her bottle vigorously. Mummy popped her head in at the door to see that everything was all right.

"Dear me—she's almost finished her bottle!" she said. "Don't bother her to finish the last few drops if she doesn't want them. Can you put her back into her cot for me and play with her for a bit till I'm ready for her?"

"Yes, I will," said Tessie. Mummy was right— Baby didn't want the last few drops, and Terry took off the bottle-teat and trickled the drops of milk into the little dolls' jug he had fetched.

"I'll go up to the kitten now," he said. "You come as soon as Mummy fetches Baby."

He ran upstairs with the little jug, and went cautiously into the boxroom. The kitten was still in the cot, but it was squirming about, wide awake, although its eyes were still fast shut.

Terry picked it up carefully, sat down on the floor, and set the tiny thing in the hollow of his crossed legs. Then he tried to feed it just as the kennel-maid had shown him. But the kitten was more lively now, and didn't seem to know that there was milk about. Terry was very glad when Tessie came up to join him.

"You hold the kitten in your hands and I'll try and open its mouth enough to get the end of the filler in," she said. And before long the kitten was eagerly drinking down the warm drops of milk that fell into its tiny mouth from the end of the glass filler.

"Goodness—isn't it hungry again!" said Terry. "I don't think it will be able to wait till Baby has her bottle at six o'clock!"

"Well, I've thought what we can do," said Tessie. "I'll go down to the kitchen and get a little milk out of the larder. And we'll keep it up here, touching the hot-water pipe, so that it will always be warm. And then we can pop in here whenever we have a minute to see if the kitten would like a meal."

"That's an *awfully* good idea!" said Terry.

The kitten was eagerly drinking

"There—the kitten's finished every drop of milk we brought up for it."

"Mummy's calling us," said Tessie. "I expect she wants us to get ready for the party. It begins at half past three, you know. I'll tuck the kitten up, and then we'll go down. And if either of us has a chance to slip up here in the middle of the party to give the kitten a drink, we will."

"You run and get some milk out of the larder,

while I go to help Mummy," said Terry. "Leave it just there, by that hot-water pipe."

He ran downstairs, and Tessie followed. She heard him talking to Mummy, and went into the kitchen. She took a small cup from the dresser and poured a little milk into it from the milk-jug. She shut the larder door carefully, and went slowly upstairs with the cup, careful not to spill even a drop.

"Here I am again, kitten!" she said, and put the cup against the hot-water pipe. "Oh—you're asleep! You do look sweet with your head on the pillow—you look like a toy kitten, not a real one!"

Then down she went to get ready for the party. What an exciting day this was!

THE party began at half past three, when boys and girls began to come up the path to the front door. The boys looked very clean and tidy, and the girls very gay in their frilly party frocks. The twins gave them a great welcome.

"It's a pity we asked Harry to the party," said Terry to Tessie, as they saw Harry coming up to the door.

"Yes—but we didn't know he was going to be so mean," said Tessie.

"How's the kitten?" said Harry, as he came up to them.

"All right. And we haven't said anything about it yet, so don't *you* say anything either," said Terry, afraid that Harry would give away their secret.

Then someone else came, and the twins had to leave Harry. Bother him! He had their ship—and their secret as well!

The party was lovely. All the children brought little presents of sweets or chocolates, and admired the lovely things that the twins had had given them. Terry did hope that Mummy wouldn't notice his big ship wasn't among them! Whatever should he say if she asked him where it was.

But she didn't. She was much too busy taking coats and hats, and then starting off the games with "Here we come gathering nuts in May!" to bother about anything else! What fun a party was!

How exciting the tea was too! Mummy had made four different kinds of sandwiches, three different kinds of cakes besides the big birthday cake, and little wobbly jellies for everyone. It was a great moment when the candles on the big cake were lighted.

"Gracious! *Eighteen!*" said little Kenneth. "Are you eighteen years old? You don't look it!"

"How's the kitten?"

"Don't you know your twice times table yet?" said Harry. "Twice times nine are eighteen! The twins are nine today. Baby!"

After tea Mummy asked if anyone wanted to wash their hands. "You take them up-stairs if they do," she said to the twins. "Then we'll play some more games."

"Tessie—now's our chance to feed the kitten again!" said Terry in a low voice. "I'll do it, shall I?"

Tessie nodded. "Yes—but don't be too long. The filler is in the cup, standing by the hot-water pipe."

Terry sped off to the little boxroom. He went in and shut the door. The kitten was squirming about in the dolls' cot, giving very small mews.

"Just coming!" Terry said to it, and went to where Tessie had stood the cup of milk by the hot pipe. He drew some into the little filler and went over to the cot. The kitten smelt the warm milk at once and mewed quite loudly. It swallowed drop after drop as Terry squeezed them out of the filler, into its tiny mouth.

"You're getting quite used to this performance, aren't you!" he said. "There! That's enough, I should think. Now I must get back to the party."

He joined the others, and gave Tessie a little nod that meant: "Yes—the kitten's fed!" and she smiled. The little creature had been at the back of her mind all the afternoon.

The party began again with musical chairs and then hunt the thimble, and then a treasure hunt, which was very exciting. Every child was given the end of a long thread and told to follow it to the other end, where he or she would find a present—but very soon the threads began to get tangled up, and then the fun began!

"I think you've all found the wrong presents!" said the twins' mother, laughing at the muddle. "But never mind—you can change presents if you like!"

Nobody wanted to go when mothers and fathers arrived to fetch their boys and girls. Soon there was only Harry left. He was always last at parties, and as no one ever fetched him, he was very difficult to get rid of! Terry was afraid he would begin to talk about the ship, and he went off and left him with Tessie.

"I must go and help Mummy with Baby," said Tessie, firmly. "Good-bye, Harry. I hope you enjoyed the party."

"Well, you didn't have fruit salad," said Harry. "And I do like fruit salad."

That was so like Harry! He went off at last and didn't even say "Thank you for a lovely time!" as all the others did.

Soon the threads began to get tangled up

Tessie flew up to the boxroom calling out to her mother that she wouldn't be a minute. Terry was already there, having just given the kitten another meal of warm milk.

"Oh good!" said Tessie. "It looks quite happy now, doesn't it, Terry. Do you think it's forgotten the shock it had this morning, when it was thrown into the pond?"

"I expect so," said Terry. "It wasn't in the water long, anyway. Mummy's calling you, Tessie. I say—wasn't it a grand party?"

"Yes, wonderful!" said Tessie, rushing off to help her mother.

"Would you like to feed Baby for me again?" said Mother. "I've rather a lot of washing up to do, and Baby is always so good with you. You do like feeding her, don't you?"

"Oh yes—feeding babies and kittens is lovely," said Tessie, before she could stop herself. Mummy was surprised.

"What do *you* know about feeding kittens?" she said, and went off to do the washing up.

"Goodness—I nearly gave our secret away!" thought Tessie. "What a good thing Terry didn't hear me—he *would* have been cross! All the same I'm sure Mummy would agree with me, if she could see our tiny kitten!"

"Well, did you enjoy your birthday?" asked Mummy, when Baby was safely in her cot again, and it was time for the twins to go to bed. Tessie gave her mother a hug.

"It was *lovely*!" she said. "From the time we woke up till this very minute. Thank you for a fine party too, Mummy—and *wasn't* our cake delicious!"

"It seemed to be," said Terry. "Harry had four pieces!"

"Go and say good night to Daddy," said Mummy, "and take some milk and biscuits up to bed with you for your supper. I'm sure you won't want anything more than that tonight, after your enormous tea!"

The twins looked at one another when she said "milk" and they both thought the same thing. They could save some for the kitten.

"What did you like best at the party?" asked Terry, as they went upstairs with their supper.

"Blowing all the eighteen candles out at once!" said Tessie. "I never thought we should! Now—just let's give the kitten its supper—and then it won't get any more until one of us wakes up in the night and goes to feed it. I hope we do—it will be so very hungry in the morning, if not!"

THE twins found the kitten fast asleep, and had to wake it to give it its "supper". It mewed as soon as it smelt the milk again. Terry stroked its soft fur.

"It was such an ugly little thing this morning," he said. "All wet and draggled—now it's sweet—but awfully thin. And I wish its back leg wasn't useless. It doesn't seem able to use it at all, when it tries to crawl."

"Perhaps that's one reason why it was thrown away," said Tessie. "Perhaps the owner didn't want to be bothered by a crippled kitten. How would *he* like it if he broke a leg or arm, and was thrown into a pond to drown, instead of being looked after in hospital till he was better!"

"Better buck up, Tessie," said Terry, "or Mummy will be up before we've undressed! Now —if either of us wakes in the night, we feed the kitten. Have you got your torch handy, because you mustn't switch on any lights? We might wake Mummy or Daddy if we do."

"We'll each slip our torches under our pillow,"

said Tessie. "Goodness me, kitten, surely you can't take any more milk! No—it's had enough now. I'll tuck it up again. I think it knows us already, don't you, Terry?"

"Well—it knows the milk-dropper all right!" said Terry, with a grin. "Give me the cup—I'll stand it by the hot pipe again. That was a brilliant idea of yours, Tessie—it just warms the milk nicely."

The twins were tired after their exciting day, and once they were in bed, they were soon asleep. Terry didn't wake once in the night—but Tessie did! She sat up in bed. Now—what had she got to remember if she woke up—oh yes—that kitten, of course.

It seemed strange in the dark little boxroom

And out of bed she slipped with her torch, and was soon cuddling the mewing kitten and feeding it with drops of milk. It seemed strange to be sitting there in the dark little boxroom, with the light from the torch streaking across the floor where she had laid it down.

"I wish I could take you into bed with me and keep you warm," she said to the kitten. "There—I'll tuck you up in the cot again. I wonder if you miss your mother. I expect she's missing *you*, and wondering where you've gone."

Terry was quite upset because he hadn't awakened in the night. They both marvelled at the kitten in the morning, because it seemed bigger already.

"I believe one of its eyes is trying to open!" said Tessie, looking at it closely. "Yes, it *is*—look, Terry—can you see a crack between its eyelids—the right eye, see?"

"Yes—it *is* opening!" said Terry. "Do you suppose it will have pink eyes, because it's a *white* kitten, Tessie? When we kept white mice, they all had pink eyes—do you remember?"

"Yes. But I don't much like pink eyes," said Tessie. "I want it to have green eyes."

"No—*blue*," said Terry. "A white kitten with

blue eyes would be lovely. Come on—we'd better go down. Mummy will soon be wondering why we keep disappearing!"

It was a good thing that it was holiday time because the twins would never have been able to feed the kitten as often as they did, if they had had to go to school each day. As it was, they had to take it out of the boxroom when a few days had gone by, because Mother suddenly said that she was going to turn out the little room and clean it.

"Turn it out?" said Tessie, startled. "But why, Mummy? It isn't untidy in there or anything, is it?"

"No. But I believe there are mice there," said Mummy. "I keep hearing little squeaks or something up on that landing, and the only place they can come from is the boxroom. I expect some mice have made a nest there of paper. I shall turn it out thoroughly tomorrow."

The twins had to make new plans for the kitten at once.

"The shed!" said Terry. "That's the only place that's safe. No one goes there but us, now Daddy has his new shed. I'll go out in the garden, Tessie, and if the coast is clear I'll whistle loudly. Then you can bring the kitten down at once. Wrap it up in a doll's shawl or something, then it will look as if it's a doll!"

Tessie ran up to the boxroom and wrapped the kitten in a little shawl. Then she heard Terry's whistle and ran downstairs. They got to the shed safely without being seen.

"Look—there's a little box here," said Terry. "Can you spare the shawl for a blanket? We could put some hay in the box under the shawl to make a nice soft bed. Did you bring the cup of milk? We shan't be able to warm it by hot-water pipes now—but perhaps it won't matter now the kitten is getting bigger."

Both the kitten's eyes were open now. They were a pale blue, and the children hoped they wouldn't turn pink. It knew them well now, and had suddenly found that it

They got to the shed

could purr! The twins were surprised when they first heard it.

"Is it feeling ill? Why is it making that funny noise?" said Tessie, anxiously.

"Silly! It's *purring* for the first time!" said Terry. "That means it's happy. What a dear little noise!"

It was beginning to crawl about too, though it still dragged one back leg behind it. Tessie felt the leg gently, but it didn't seem to be broken. Perhaps it would get right.

It was a good thing that Tessie had taken the kitten out of the boxroom straight away—because Mummy changed her mind and turned it out that very morning.

"But I didn't find any mice!" she said. "All the same I found something rather *peculiar* in the box-room."

"What?" asked the twins.

"Your new dolls' cot, Tessie!" said Mummy. "Whatever was it doing in there? Did your baby doll cry at night and wake you—and so you put her there?"

That made the twins laugh. Terry changed the subject, afraid that Tessie wouldn't be able to explain about the dolls' cot and would go red, and make Mummy curious. They *couldn't* let the kitten be given away to anyone now—they really couldn't. And Mummy might say it would have to go, if she found out about it. But how could *anyone* help liking it—it really was the prettiest little thing now.

The days went by, and the kitten still lived in the shed, and the twins still fed it regularly. Once or twice they gave it bits of fish they had saved from their own dinner, and it gobbled them up. It had two rows of very small, pointed teeth, and big blue eyes.

"They're going to turn green, I think," said Terry. "It will be a lovely cat then—pure white with bright green eyes!"

"You know—we've never given it a name yet," said Tessie, rolling it over and over, and tickling its tummy. "What shall we call it?"

"I don't know," said Terry. "It's got fine whiskers—shall we call it Whiskers? Or Purry because it's always purring?"

"No. Those aren't *very* good names," said Tessie. "Oh, look at it—it's rolled itself up into a white ball, and it's fighting its tail. It's like a round ball of snow!"

"*That's* its name—Snowy!" said Terry, at once. "Snowy—you'll have to learn your name! Snowy!"

"Miaow!" said Snowy, and ran to Terry.

"There!" he said. "You know your name already, don't you, Snowy?"

9.   "YOU'RE THE
MEANEST BOY IN THE WORLD"

THAT Saturday something very awkward happened. Daddy announced that he would like to sail Terry's birthday ship with him!

"We'll take it down to the pond," he said. "There's a little breeze and the ship would sail well."

But *Harry* still had the ship! He wouldn't give it back, though Terry had asked him many times.

"No," he said, each time. "As long as I keep your secret about the kitten, you've got to lend me your ship. If you take it back I'll tell about the kitten."

"You're horrible and mean and unkind," said Terry. He didn't like to see Tessie looking so troubled. But Harry only laughed.

And oh dear—now Daddy wanted to go and sail the ship that very afternoon!

Terry hunted about in his mind for some good excuse.

"Oh Daddy—it's a long way to the pond, and it looks like rain," he said, going very red.

"And Mummy asked me to take Baby in her

pram to see Granny," said Tessie, quite truthfully.

"Well, *you* can take Baby, and Terry can come with me," said Daddy. "A long way to the pond! I never heard such nonsense! Don't you *want* to come, Terry?"

"Oh *yes!*" said poor Terry. "I love going anywhere with you, Daddy, you know that!"

"Well, we'll go then," said Daddy. "Go and get your ship, and we'll have a look at her, and see if she's properly rigged."

Terry looked at Tessie in despair. Harry had the ship, so he couldn't *possibly* go and get it. Daddy was puzzled.

"Well, Terry, please go along and get it," he said, sounding impatient. "I should have thought you'd have loved the chance of sailing that lovely ship. I don't believe you've sailed it more than once, have you? I must say I've been rather surprised."

Terry didn't know what to do. He turned as if to go and get his ship. Tessie looked frightened, because she was sure that Daddy was soon going to be very angry!

Terry turned round again, his face as red as fire. "I can't go and get it, Daddy," he said. "It's not here."

"Well, where is it, then?" said Daddy, astonished.

"Er—I lent it to Harry—you know, the vet's son," stammered Terry. "He—he loves ships too."

"You lent that beautiful ship to *Harry*—that careless fellow!" cried his father. "Whatever possessed you to do that! Go and get it back at once."

"Well—you see," began Terry, and then didn't say any more, because that would have meant giving away the secret of the little white kitten. He stared miserably at his father.

"Well, either *you* go and get your ship back, or *I* go and get it," said Daddy. "And if *I* get it, I shall tell Master Harry what I think of him, for borrowing that beautiful ship. I told him he was *not* to borrow anything more from you, after he left those beautiful animal books of yours out in the rain all night."

"I'll go and get the ship," said Terry, at once. Harry would certainly give away the secret if Daddy went! He set off at once, hoping that Harry would not be mean. After all, he had had that lovely ship for ages now!

Harry *was* mean!

"You said I could have your ship as long as I

kept your secret," he said. "And I'm *still* keeping your secret, so I shall still keep your ship. Of course, if you don't *want* me to keep your secret any longer, I won't."

Terry stared at him, clenching his fists. He wanted to fight Harry at that moment. Harry saw the clenched fists and laughed.

"Of course, you can have your ship just for today, but you'll have to pay me fifty pence."

"You're the meanest boy in the whole world," said Terry, fiercely. He put his hand in his pocket and took out the Saturday money that his father had given him that morning. He slammed it down on the top of the wall.

"There you are! There's your money —now give me my ship!"

Harry moved towards the money, but Terry clapped his hand over it.

"No, you don't! You won't *touch*

"Pay me fifty pence"

my fifty pence until I have my ship," he said.

Harry laughed and went into his house. He brought out the ship and handed it to Terry, snatching the money as he did so.

"You've tangled up all the rigging," said Terry angrily. "And you've dented the keel."

"That was done when you lent it to me," said Harry at once.

"Fibber!" said Terry, disgusted, and went off with his ship. How he detested Harry! Just because he and Tessie had wanted help for a half-drowned kitten, Harry had got him into all this trouble. Whatever would Daddy say when he saw the tangled rigging and bent keel?

Daddy had a great deal to say about the ship! He was very cross indeed.

"To think you've let this lovely ship get into this state in such a short time!" he said. "Or did Harry do it? Yes, I suppose he did. Why in the world you lent it to him I don't know! You know I don't like you to have much to do with Harry— he's not a good friend for you. I'm very disappointed in you, Terry. I'm afraid it will take so long to get the ship ready for sailing that it's not worth while our going."

Terry couldn't bear to have his father so

disappointed in him. "I'm very sorry, Daddy," he said.

"Well, look—go and buy some new string, and we'll rig the whole ship again," said Daddy. "I gave you your fifty pence piece this morning, didn't I?"

Terry put his hand into his pocket—and then remembered that he had given it to Harry, so that he might get his ship back. Good gracious! Now he couldn't even buy the string.

"Now don't say you've spent all your money already," said Daddy. "You know you're supposed to save ten pence a week in your money box. Have you put that into it?"

"No, Daddy," said Terry.

"Well, do you mean to say you've spent it all?" said Daddy. "Not even a penny left?"

"I've got a penny from last week," said Terry, desperately, and took it out. He simply didn't know *what* to say.

Tessie had been listening to all this, frightened and unhappy. She went to Terry, holding out her own fifty pence.

"Terry can have *my* money," she said. "I've plenty in my money box. You go and buy the string, Terry."

"No," said Daddy, giving the ship back to Terry. "No. I don't feel as if I want to take Terry out with me today. I feel rather ashamed of him." And he went indoors without another word.

Poor Terry. He stared at Tessie, and then, afraid that he might cry, he rushed into the little shed, almost falling over Snowy the kitten. "What a thing to happen!" he said to the surprised kitten. "NOW what am I to do?"

D ADDY wasn't at all pleased with Terry all that day and for several days afterwards. Mummy heard about the spoilt ship too, and was sad to think that Terry had lent it to Harry.

"I should have thought that you valued it too much to lend it to anyone before Daddy had even sailed it with you," she said. "You'll have to be specially good and helpful the next week or two, so that Daddy won't feel so disappointed in you."

Both the twins were miserable, and, to make things worse, Harry was angry because Terry didn't bring the ship back again.

"I can't," said Terry. "And I warn you, if I do, my father will come round and get it back—and you'll get some pretty hard things said to you. My father doesn't think much of you."

So Harry didn't dare to say much more. He was afraid of Terry's father! But he kept hinting that he was going to call in and see their mother.

"And I'll ask her how the kitten is getting on," he said. "Shall I?"

Snowy was getting on famously! It was a

beautiful little creature now. Its eyes were no longer blue, but as green as cucumbers, and very wide and bright. The only thing wrong with it was its back leg, which still dragged a little, though the kitten could run quite fast on the other three. It could jump too, and the twins laughed to see it pouncing after a cotton reel they had tied to a bit of string.

Nobody knew it lived in the shed. When Mummy took Baby out for a walk in her pram, the twins let the kitten out and it played on the grass like a mad thing. It drank quite a lot of milk now, and ate the bits of bread too that Tessie put to soak in the milk. Sometimes, for a treat, it had odd bits of fish or pudding that the children saved for it from their own plates.

"What shall we do when it gets any bigger?" said Terry. "We can't keep it shut up all the time!"

"Oh dear—I don't know," said Tessie, taking the kitten into her arms. "Look, Terry—there's a jackdaw down on the lawn again. I wonder if it's the one that flew off with Mummy's thimble the other day."

"Yes—that was annoying of it!" said Terry, watching the big jackdaw strutting about on the grass. "Did you see it take it?"

"Yes," said Tessie. "Mummy had been sewing out here in the summer-house, watching Baby nearby in her pram. She went indoors to answer the telephone and left me with Baby. And suddenly the jackdaw flew into the summer-house, perched on the wooden table there, and then flew off with Mummy's best silver thimble!"

"And Mummy says that it must have seen her best brooch winking in the sun on her dressing-table," said Terry, "because that suddenly disappeared too. Daddy says that jackdaws love to take bright things."

The big black jackdaw strutted about, prying under bushes, and pecking at a worm on the grass. And then, quite suddenly Snowy leapt out of Tessie's arms and raced over

"Chack-chack-chack!"

the lawn, its bad leg dragging a little as it ran!

The kitten was almost on the jackdaw before the big bird even saw it. With a loud "chack-chack-chack!" the jackdaw rose in the air, and flew away at once. The children laughed at the kitten's surprise.

"You'll have to get used to birds flying off into the air!" said Terry. "You brave little thing! The bird was much bigger than you!"

Snowy was very playful indeed. He grew more beautiful every day, and had a magnificent coat of soft, very white fur. He had learnt to wash himself now, and spent a long time keeping himself as white as snow. He knew his name and came running to the door of the shed, mewing loudly, as soon as he heard the twins coming, calling to him in a low voice.

His mew became so loud that the twins began to be afraid Mummy would hear him when she came into the garden to put Baby's pram out in the sun.

Terry felt worried. "I'm afraid that as I'm still in disgrace with Daddy, he'll be really *angry* if he finds out we've been keeping a kitten in secret," he said. "Then what will happen to Snowy?"

"He'll be sent away somewhere," said Tessie,

looking ready to cry. "And he'll be so unhappy because he loves us now."

Well, of course, a kitten can't be kept secret for ever, and a day came when Snowy was discovered! It happened very suddenly.

Mummy was sitting out on the lawn with Baby on a rug beside her, kicking merrily. Her next door neighbour, Mrs. Janes, called to her over the wall.

"How's that bonny baby of yours?"

Mummy left her deck-chair, and went over to the wall to have a little chat. And then, on big black wings, the jackdaw came flying down on the grass! It saw Baby Anne lying there kicking, and it caught sight of something shining brightly in her hand—her new silver rattle!

"Chack!" said the jackdaw, delighted to see the glittering thing, and it strutted up to the baby. It pecked at the silver rattle, but the baby wouldn't let go, staring at the black bird with big, frightened eyes. The jackdaw pecked again, and the baby yelled.

Mummy turned round at once, and saw the pecking jackdaw. She gave a scream—but before she could move towards the baby, someone else was there!

It pecked at the silver rattle

Snowy the kitten had seen the jackdaw from the window of his shed half-way down the garden. His sharp eyes watched the bird as it went over to the baby—and then, scrambling and pushing, the kitten forced open the little window and leapt down, landing with a bump that really surprised him. He got back his breath and raced on three legs over to the rug where the baby lay, with the jackdaw at the shining rattle.

Snowy leapt at the big bird—and with a frightened "chack-chack!" the jackdaw rose into the air, leaving one black feather in the kitten's mouth!

And then Mummy was there, picking up Baby Anne, and comforting her.

"There, there!" she said. "Naughty bird to

come and frighten Baby! And good gracious me—
WHERE did this brave little kitten come from? It
just scared the jackdaw away before it pecked *you*,
Baby!"

She sat down with Baby Anne on the rug, and
the kitten crept on to her skirt and lay there.
Mummy stroked it. "You dear, pretty little thing!
Whom do you belong to?"

At that moment the twins ran down the garden
to tell Mummy about the shopping they had just
been doing—and HOW surprised they were to see
Mummy petting the little white kitten! They stood
still in amazement.

"Look, darlings!" said Mummy. "Look at this
little pet of a kitten! That jackdaw came down and
saw Baby's shining silver rattle, and began to peck
at it, and frightened Baby—and this tiny thing
appeared from somewhere and drove the bird
away. I do wonder who it belongs to. Isn't it
sweet?"

"Yes—it's very sweet," said Tessie, not know-
ing what to say. "It's a darling."

"We must find out who the owner is," said
Mummy. "You can fetch the kitten a saucer of
milk—it really did save Baby from being badly
pecked. Dear me—how I wish it was *our* kitten! I

wouldn't mind having one like this, I really wouldn't!"

The twins could hardly believe their ears! "Mummy! Do you mean that?" said Terry at once. "Do you *really* wish it was ours?"

"Yes," said Mummy. "It's a most lovable little thing—look at it cuddling up to me. Do you know whose it is?"

"Yes," said Tessie. "Yes, we do know. It's *ours*, Mummy. Terry's and mine! Oh—please do say we can keep it!"

"AND NOW
IT'S REALLY OURS!"

WHEN Mummy heard Tessie say that the kitten belonged to her and Terry, she couldn't believe her ears. She stared at the excited twins in astonishment.

"Now what exactly do you mean?" she said. "The kitten *can't* be yours! I've never seen it before! Tell me all about it, please."

So, taking the kitten on to her knee, Tessie told her mother how they had rescued the little thing from drowning, and how they had gone to ask Harry if he could help it, because his father was a vet.

"And that's when I had to lend Harry my ship," said Terry, "because he wouldn't help us with the kitten unless I did! Miss Morgan, the kennel-maid, told us how to look after it."

"We couldn't tell you because we knew you didn't want a puppy or kitten till Baby could walk," said Tessie. "But Mummy, it was such a poor, poor little kitten, so wet and cold and thin and hungry, we simply *had* to take it home."

"Darling Tessie," said Mummy, and put her

arm round the little girl. "I'm glad you did that. I'd have done it too! Poor little kitten—how could anyone be so cruel! And to think that, small as it was, it chased that big jackdaw away! Why, it might have pecked Baby very badly!"

"Mummy—do you really like the kitten then?" asked Terry, eagerly. "*Will* you keep it? It is growing big now and it was getting so difficult to hide it. You did say you wished it was ours, didn't you?"

"Yes, I did. And I meant it," said Mummy, stroking Snowy gently. "What a beautiful little creature it is! But we must do something about its leg. Perhaps Daddy will take it to the vet."

"Do you think Daddy will still feel disappointed in me, when he knows it was because of the kitten that I had to lend my new ship to Harry?" asked Terry, anxiously.

"He'll be *proud* of you, Terry, I promise you that!" said Mummy. "You're two good kind children, and *any* mother would be proud of you. We'll tell Daddy as soon as ever he comes home. Oh *look* at the kitten—it's cuddling up in my skirt again. It really *does* belong to us, doesn't it!"

The twins were very, very happy. Secrets were fun—but this one had become very worrying, especially after Daddy had found out about the ship being lent to Harry. It was lovely to feel that the kitten could be with them now whenever they wanted it.

"We'll be very careful not to let Snowy get under your feet, Mummy," said Tessie. "I'll put

"It really does belong to us"

him into my room whenever I know you've got to carry Baby anywhere."

"Oh, it seems such a sensible little thing, I'm sure it won't trip me up," said Mummy, who really did think Snowy was wonderful. "I'm longing to tell Daddy all about it."

Daddy was *most* astonished when he heard the story. He sat and listened as the twins and Mummy told him all about it, shaking his head in amazement.

"A kitten! And it's been here such a long time and we never guessed!" he said. "No wonder Mummy thought there were mice squeaking in the boxroom! Let me hold it—it looks a pet."

The kitten sniffed at Daddy's hands and then settled down on his knee, purring loudly.

"There! It knows it belongs to you too, Daddy," said Tessie, delighted. "Hark at it telling you!"

"I understand about the ship now, Terry," said Daddy, stroking Snowy. "And although I scolded you hard about it, I think it was kind of you to give up something you were proud of in order to get help for the kitten. I shall have a few words to say to Harry about that, though!"

"There's something wrong with its leg," said Mummy. "It drags that back one a bit, Daddy. We must have it seen to before it gets stiff for always."

"We'll take it straight round to the vet this very minute," said Daddy. "I'll telephone to him to say we're coming. Hold the kitten, Terry."

"Daddy—you're not disappointed in me any more, are you?" said Terry, anxious that everything should be absolutely right between him and his father now. It had worried him very much to feel that his father wasn't proud of him.

"Disappointed! I'm only sorry I didn't understand what was happening," said Daddy, clapping Terry on the back. "I wouldn't have scolded you at all, you know that. I'm prouder of you—and Tessie too—than I ever was before!"

Daddy, Terry and Tessie took the kitten round to the vet. He was kind and gentle, and examined the stiff little leg carefully.

"Leave it with me tonight," he said. "I shall have to manipulate it a little—I can put it right, but I may have to put the kitten to sleep while I do it. When it wakes up, its leg will hurt it a little —but it will be quite all right in a few days!"

"Oh, *thank* you!" said Tessie, delighted. "Isn't it a lovely kitten, Mr. Williams?"

"It's a beauty!" said the vet, stroking it. "I can't think how anyone could have been foolish enough, as well as unkind enough, to throw it into a pond—it's a kitten that could win a prize any day, when it grows up. I suppose they didn't want a kitten with a bad leg! Leave it with me now."

"Thank you," said the twins' father. "Now— may I have a word with your boy Harry, please? Where is he?"

"In the garden somewhere," said the vet. "Will you tell my next patient to come in please, as you go out? And don't worry about the kitten. It will be as right as rain tomorrow!"

They all went out. "Call Harry," said Daddy to Terry. "Look—there he is!"

Terry called loudly. "Harry! Harry, you're wanted!"

Harry came running up eagerly, hoping that he could perhaps get some more money out of Terry. He stopped very suddenly when he saw the twins' father.

"Come here, please, Harry," said Daddy. "I've

something to say to you. No—don't run away—unless you'd rather I said it to your father."

That made Harry come back at once, his face as red as a beetroot. He stood sulkily on the garden path.

"Take that scowl off your face," said

"Come here, Harry"

the twins' father. "You know what I want to say to you, don't you? I know all about your mean behaviour over the ship, and how you made Terry give you his money. I shall not tell your father this time—but NEXT time, there will be serious trouble. Do you understand?"

"I'll—I'll give back the fifty pence," mumbled Harry, very scared indeed. "Don't tell my father. He'll thrash me. I'll go and get the money now."

"You can give it to Terry tomorrow," said the twins' father. "He will be coming to fetch the kitten—and remember—any more of this kind of thing, and you'll find yourself really in trouble!"

They went out of the gate and left Harry shaking in his shoes. Goodness—to think that the twins' *father* knew all about his meanness! Harry made up his mind to turn over a new leaf at once, in case his *own* father got to hear of it!

It was a happy little family that went home that evening. The twins hung on to their father's arm, and told him every single thing about the kitten.

"And now it's to be *really* ours!" said Tessie, happily. "Oh, I do hope its leg will soon be better. Won't Baby love it when she's a bit bigger, Daddy?"

"Oh, we shall all love it!" said Daddy. "It looks as if Snowy will be the happiest kitten in the world. But how you managed to keep your secret so well, I really do not know!"

12. "ONE GOOD TURN DESERVES ANOTHER — PURR–PURR–PURR!"

NEXT morning the twins went to fetch the kitten from the vet's. Harry was at the gate, waiting for them. "Here's the money," he said, and pushed it into Terry's hand. "I'm sorry for what I did." And then away he went before they could say a word.

"Hallo, twins!" called Miss Morgan, the kennel-maid. "The vet's gone out to see to a horse that's had an accident. Here's your kitten—my word, hasn't it grown since you first brought it here! It's a beauty!"

"What about its leg?" asked Tessie, anxiously, stroking Snowy as he lay in the kennel-maid's arms.

"Quite all right," said Miss Morgan. "It will feel a bit bruised for a day or two—so don't be surprised if he still limps a little. But he will soon run on all four legs, and, if I know anything about it, he will be a regular little rascal!"

"Dear little Snowy!" said Tessie, and the kitten looked at her out of big green eyes, and purred loudly as she took it from Miss Morgan. "You're going to belong to the whole family now, instead of just to Terry and me."

"You know, this kitten must have come from quite a good litter of kittens," said Miss Morgan. "It's a real beauty. If I were you, I'd enter it for the Kitten Section of the Cat Show when it's held in a few weeks. It might win a prize for you."

"Really?" said Terry, in delight. "Do you hear that, Snowy? You might win a prize—how would you like that?"

The kitten mewed, and Miss Morgan laughed.

"It says it would like it very much, if it's something to eat!" she said. "Well good-bye now—I've about twelve pups to see to, and a few cats—a guinea-pig and some rabbits. I must go and see to my big family at once!"

In two days' time the kitten's leg was perfectly strong, and it could run on all fours, instead of only on three legs. Now that Mummy knew about it, it had the free run of the house, and was soon at home everywhere. Baby Anne loved it—and when Mummy put it on her pram for her to play with, it was as gentle as could be, and didn't put out one single claw. Mummy didn't fall over it once—even though it liked to hide under beds and chairs and leap out at any passing feet.

"It's really quite easy to watch out for it," said Mummy. "I was silly not to let you have one before. We might perhaps have a puppy next, while Snowy is still a kitten. Then they could grow up together!"

"For Christmas, Mummy!" said the twins, both together. "A black one, and we'll call it Sooty," added Terry. "Snowy and Sooty—that would be fun!"

One day Daddy took Terry down to the river to sail his ship—and how beautifully it sailed there, tugging at its string. All its rigging had been renewed, and the keel had been mended. Terry was very proud when he saw so many boys coming up to watch the *Flying Swan*.

On the way home Terry spotted a big notice in a shop.

"Look, Daddy!" he said. "The Cat Show is on next month, and there's a class for kittens. Miss Morgan said Snowy was a fine kitten and we ought to put him into the Cat Show. Can we? Do let's!"

"Well, of course," said Daddy. "I'll be very surprised if there's a prettier kitten than our Snowy! WHAT a good thing you were sailing your ship on the pond, when the poor little thing was thrown into the water!"

"Yes—and how surprised that person would be if he—or she—could see the kitten now!" said Terry. "Quick, let's get back home and tell Tessie about the Cat Show."

Tessie was very excited. She picked up Snowy and patted him. "We'll brush you, and give you a lovely green ribbon to match your eyes!" she said. "Do try and win a prize, Snowy, even if it's only a little one! We'd be prouder still of you then!"

By the time the Cat Show came, Snowy was the funniest, most mischievous kitten that any of them had ever seen. Daddy said he had never laughed so much in his life as he had since Snowy arrived in the family.

"He saw himself in the mirror yesterday," said Daddy, "and thought it was another cat there. So he tried to make friends with it, and purred loudly, and patted the glass. Then when the kitten in the mirror wouldn't make friends, he flew at it and tried to bite it—and couldn't think why he got his nose bumped so hard!"

On the day of the Show Tessie brushed Snowy till his coat gleamed like the snow itself. Then she tied a green ribbon round his neck to match his eyes.

"You look good enough to have your picture on a chocolate box!" she said. "Mummy, isn't he lovely? Do you think he will win a prize? We've entered him in the 'White Kitten' class and the 'Prettiest Kitten' class as well."

"He won't get a prize in the 'White Kitten' class," said Mummy, "because usually kittens belonging to Prize Pedigree Cats win those prizes. But he might win a Prettiest Kitten prize. You have certainly made him look very fine, Tessie!"

Very proudly the children carried Snowy to the Cat Show in a closed basket with a handle. They entered his name in the White Kitten Class and the Prettiest Kitten class too. He was put in a cage alongside many other cages of kittens—and, how strange, next to him was a white kitten almost EXACTLY like him! The man in charge of it stared at Snowy in surprise.

"Where did you get that kitten?" he said. "It might be the twin of mine!"

Terry told him. "Somebody threw it into the pond to drown it, and we rescued it. It had a bad leg, poor little thing, and we think that was why it was thrown away."

"A bad leg!" said the man, and turned and said something to the boy with him. Terry couldn't help hearing what he said. "Do you suppose that's the one we didn't want, because of the leg, Leonard? It's the living image of ours here—green eyes and all!"

"Sh!" said the boy, and frowned at the man. "They'll hear you!"

The twins *had* heard, of course, and they looked at one another in disgust. Was *this* the boy who had tried to drown their kitten?

Soon the judges came along—and they exclaimed in delight when they saw Snowy. And then they saw the white kitten in the next cage, so exactly like him. They examined them both carefully, and scribbled notes on their cards. Then they passed on.

And will you believe it, when the prize-winners' names were called out over the microphone, Snowy had won *both* the Kitten Prizes—first prize in the White Kitten class, and the first prize in the Prettiest Kitten one as well. The twins could hardly believe their ears!

"Did you hear that, Snowy?" said Tessie, putting her hand into the kitten's cage and stroking its soft fur. "You've won *two* prizes. You've beaten all the other kittens!"

The man and the boy who owned the kitten in

the next cage were angry, for they thought their own kitten would easily win. They glared at Snowy.

"Just because its eyes are greener than our kitten's!" said the boy. "I wish I'd drowned it properly."

"Well, it serves you right," said Tessie, unexpectedly, remembering again the tiny, wet,

"It—just—serves—you—RIGHT!"

frightened little thing that Terry had rescued from the pond. "It—just—serves—you—RIGHT!"

"I don't know what you're talking about, you silly little girl," said the man. But he did, of course!

The twins carried Snowy home in triumph, and

the prizes too. Two whole pounds, one for each win—and cards to say that Snowy was the "Best White Kitten in Show" and the "Prettiest Kitten in Show" as well.

"We'll buy you a lovely basket of your own, with a cushion inside," said Tessie, joyfully. "Won't Mummy be pleased at the news!"

She was! She cuddled Snowy, and he patted her with his tiny paw. "You shall certainly have a new basket for your very own," she said, and the kitten mewed loudly, and purred.

"What did you say?" said Mummy. "Oh—you want Tessie to buy herself a pretty brooch—and Terry to buy a new railway signal for his electric train? Well, that's kind of you, Snowy. I'll give them back a pound of your prize money—here it is, twins!"

"But—do you suppose Snowy *really* wants us to do that?" said Tessie, pleased.

"Of course! He loves you, doesn't he?" said Mummy. "And I'm sure I know what he's purring to you this very minute. Listen! Can't you hear him purring, 'One good turn deserves another, one good turn deserves another, purr-purr-purr!'"

Snowy jumped on to Tessie's shoulder and purred in her ear, rubbing his head against her—

and then he jumped on to Terry's and did exactly the same!

"He's telling us again!" said Tessie. "All right, Snowy—we'll share your prize-money. Thank you VERY much! Oh Mummy—don't you wish some-

Snowy jumped on to Tessie's shoulder

one could tell the story of our Birthday Kitten? I do!"

Well—I've told it—and now there's nothing more to say except a few words from Snowy himself. "Purr-rr-rr-rr-rr!"

THE BOY WHO WANTED A DOG

Enid Blyton

Donald desperately wanted a dog of his own, but his parents wouldn't permit it. Instead, he was allowed to go to the local vet's kennels to help look after the dogs there – but even that is stopped when his father discovers that it interferes with his homework.

The saddest little boy in the world, Donald goes to the kennels for one last time . . .